William Winter

Thistle-down

A Book of Lyrics

William Winter

Thistle-down
A Book of Lyrics

ISBN/EAN: 9783744766067

Printed in Europe, USA, Canada, Australia, Japan

Cover: Foto ©Andreas Hilbeck / pixelio.de

More available books at **www.hansebooks.com**

THISTLE-DOWN:

𝔄 𝔅𝔬𝔬𝔨 𝔬𝔣 𝔏𝔶𝔯𝔦𝔠𝔰.

BY

WILLIAM WINTER.

LONDON:

TINSLEY BROTHERS, 8 CATHERINE ST., STRAND.

1878.

To

Joseph Jefferson.

———◦———

My dear Jefferson,

You and I, for many years, have been comrades in heart and thought. It will be my lasting honour if, through this Book, which I dedicate to you, we are also, though only for a day, comrades in name.

William Winter.

New York, Oct. 29th, 1877.

CONTENTS.

viii CONTENTS.

HOMAGE.

WHITE daisies on the meadow green
        Present thy beauteous form to me:
Peaceful and joyful these are seen,
        And peace and joy encompass thee.
I watch them where they dance and shine,
And love them—for their beauty's thine.

Red roses o'er the woodland brook
        Remember me thy lovely face:
So blushing and so fresh its look,
        So wild and shy its radiant grace.
I kiss them, in their coy retreat,
And think of lips more soft and sweet.

Gold arrows of the merry morn,
        Shot swiftly over Eastern seas;
Gold tassels of the bending corn
        That ripple in the August breeze,
Thy wildering smile, thy glorious hair,
And all thy power and state declare.

B

HOMAGE.

White, red, and gold—the awful crown
    Of virtue and of beauty too!
From what a height those eyes look down
    On him who proudly dares to sue!
Yet, free from self as God from sin
Is love that loves, nor asks to win.

Let me but love thee in the flower,
    The waving grass, the dancing wave,
The fragrant pomp of garden bower,
    The violet on the nameless grave,
Sweet dreams by night, sweet thoughts by day,
And time shall tire ere love decay.

Let me but love thee in the glow
    When morning on the ocean shines,
Or in the mighty winds that blow
    Snow-laden through the mountain pines—
In all that's fair, or grand, or dread,
And all shall die ere love be dead.

MY QUEEN.

HE loves not well whose love is bold!
    I would not have thee come too nigh.
The sun's gold would not seem pure gold
    Unless the sun were in the sky:
To take him thence and chain him near
Would make his beauty disappear.

He keeps his state,—do thou keep thine,
    And shine upon me from afar!
So shall I bask in light divine,
    That falls from love's own guiding star;
So shall thy eminence be high,
And so my passion shall not die.

But all my life shall reach its hands
    Of lofty longing toward thy face,
And be as one who speechless stands
    In rapture at some perfect grace.
My love, my hope, my all, shall be
To look to heaven and look to thee.

Thy eyes shall be the heavenly lights;
    Thy voice shall be the summer breeze,
What time it sways, on moonlit nights,
    The murmuring tops of leafy trees;
And I will touch thy beauteous form
In June's red roses rich and warm.

But thou thyself shalt come not down
    From that pure region far above;
But keep thy throne and wear thy crown,
    Queen of my heart and queen of love!
A monarch in thy realm complete,
And I a monarch—at thy feet!

THE CHOICE.

THE stroller in the pensive field
    Doth many a wildering flower descry:
Sometimes to him the roses yield;
    Sometimes the lilies feed his eye;
Sometimes he takes delight in one,
Sometimes in all, sometimes in none.

But when, in dusky woodland ways,
    He sees, beside some dreaming stone,
The fresh untutored violet raise
    Her pleading eyes for him alone,
Then makes his heart its final choice,
And nature speaks in passion's voice.

The stroller beauty's garden through,—
    By many a wayward impulse led,—
Sometimes is charmed by gold and blue,
    Sometimes by brown and mantling red;
Sometimes proud dame and maiden small
Please just the same, or not at all.

But when, remote from pleasure's whirl,
 He sees, at home's sequestered shrine,
The ardent, cheerful, guileless girl,
 Of mortal mould, but soul divine,—
Too good, too beautiful, to know
How fair her worth and beauty show;

Then all his roving fancies pause,
 Entranced by this o'erwhelming grace;
It rules him by celestial laws,
 It lights a splendour in his face:
'Tis the best good that Fate can give:
He wins it—and begins to live.

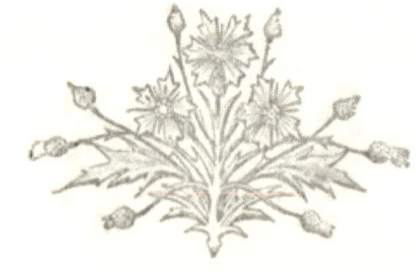

THE QUESTION.

BECAUSE love's sigh is but a sigh,
　　Doth it the less love's heart disclose?
Because the rose must fade and die,
　　Is it the less the lovely rose?
Because black night must shroud the day,
Shall the brave sun no more be gay?

Because chill autumn frights the birds,
　　Shall we distrust that spring will come?
Because sweet words are only words,
　　Shall love for evermore be dumb?
Because our bliss is fleeting bliss,
Shall we who love forbear to kiss?

Because those eyes of gentle mirth
　　Must sometime cease my heart to thrill.
Because the sweetest voice on earth
　　Sooner or later must be still,
Because its idol is unsure,
Shall my strong love the less endure?

Ah, no! let lovers breathe their sighs,
    And roses bloom, and music sound,
And passion burn on lips and eyes,
    And pleasure's merry world go round :
Let golden sunshine flood the sky,
And let me love, or let me die!

THE IDEAL.

ER young face is good and fair,
    Lily-white and rosy-red;
And the brown and silken hair
    Hovers, mist-like, round her head.

And her voice is soft and low,
    Clear as music and as sweet;
Hearing it, you hardly know
    Where the sound and silence meet.

All the magic who can tell
    Of her laughter and her sighs?
Or what heavenly meanings dwell
    In her kind, confiding eyes?

Pretty lips, as rubies bright,
    Scarcely hide the tiny pearls;
Little wandering stars of light
    Love to nestle in her curls.

All her ways are winning ways,
  Full of tenderness and grace ;
And a witching sweetness plays
  Fondly o'er her gentle face.

True and pure her soul within,—
  Breathing a celestial air !
Evil and the shame of sin
  Could not dwell a moment there.

Is it but a vision, this ?
  Fond creation of the brain ?
Phantom of a fancied bliss ?
  Type of beauty void and vain ?

No ! the tides of being roll
  Toward a heaven that's yet to be,
Where this idol of my soul
  Waits and longs for love and me !

THE TRIUMPH.

SURGE up in wanton waves to-day,
    Ye memories of a restless Past!
In shine and shadow glance and play,—
    This golden moment is your last.

Float, Phantoms, o'er a sapphire sea,—
    Remembered joy, remembered pain,
Passions and fears that used to be,
    But never can be mine again.

Sweet Visions, faded long ago,
    So beautiful, and once so dear,—
That wrought my bliss, that wrought my woe,—
    Your welcome and farewell are here.

For now no more can fancy wile
    My steadfast soul with dreams untrue.
I give you each a parting smile,
    I give you all a glad adieu.

Henceforth, for me, the Past is dead,
  And sunken deep in Lethe's waves.
Firm is the ground whereon I tread,
  That will not know the shape of graves.

As one whose soul, in second birth,
  Attains its natural height and scope,
I spurn away the dust of earth,
  I scale the radiant peaks of hope.

The sunshine wraps me in its arms,
  North winds of power around me blow,
And heaven's ablaze with starry charms
  To bless the path whereon I go.

For mine is now the ardent truth
  And secret of the lover's kiss;
The valley of immortal youth;
  The sacred mountain-height of bliss.

THE ANCHOR.

THINK of me as your friend, I pray,
　　And call me by a loving name:
I will not care what others say,
　　If only you remain the same.
I will not care how dark the night,
　　I will not care how wild the storm:
Your love will fill my heart with light,
　　And shield me close and keep me warm.

Think of me as your friend, I pray,
　　For else my life is little worth:
So shall your memory light my way,
　　Although we meet no more on earth.
For while I know your faith secure,
　　I ask no happier fate to see;
Thus to be loved by one so pure
　　Is honour rich enough for me.

THE REQUIEM.

———

BRING withered autumn leaves,
 Call everything that grieves,
And build a funeral pyre above his head!
 Heap there all golden promise that deceives,
 Beauty that wins the heart, and then bereaves,—
  For Love is dead.

 Not slowly did he die.
 A meteor from the sky
Falls not so swiftly as his spirit fled,
 When, with regretful, half-averted eye,
 He gave one little smile, one little sigh,
  And so was sped.

 But O, not yet, not yet
 Would my lost soul forget
How beautiful he was while he did live,
 Or, when his eyes were dewy and lips wet,
 What kisses, tenderer than all regret,
  My love would give.

Strew roses on his breast,
　He loved the roses best;
He never cared for lilies or for snow.
　　Let be this bitter end of his sweet quest;
　　Let be the pallid silence that is rest—
　　　　And let all go!

RELICS.

THE violets that you gave are dead—
 They could not bear the loss of you:
The spirit of the rose has fled—
 It loved you, and its love was true:
Back to your lips that spirit flies,
To bask beneath your radiant eyes.

Only the ashes bide with me,
 The ashes of the ruined flowers—
Types of a rapture not to be,
 Sad relics of bewildering hours,
Poor, frail, forlorn, and piteous shows
Of errant passion's wasted woes.

He grandly loves who loves in vain:
 These withered flowers that lesson teach.
They suffered, they did not complain,
 Their life was love too great for speech.
In silent pride their fate they bore;
They loved, they grieved, they died—no more!

Far off the purple banners flare,
   Beneath the golden morning spread :
I know what queen is worshipped there,
   What laurels wreathe her lovely head.
Her name be sacred in my thought,
And sacred be the grief she brought.

For, since I saw that glorious face,
   And heard the music of that voice,
Much beauty's fallen to disgrace
   That used to make my heart rejoice ;
And rose and violet ne'er can be
The same that once they were to me.

THE BALLAD OF CONSTANCE.

WITH diamond dew the grass was wet,—
    'Twas in the Spring and gentlest weather,—
And all the birds of morning met,
    And carolled in her heart together.

The wind blew softly o'er the land,
    And softly kissed the joyous ocean;
He walked beside her on the sand,
    And gave and won a heart's devotion.

The thistledown was in the breeze,
    With birds of passage homeward flying;
His fortune lured him o'er the seas,
    And on the shore he left her, sighing.

She saw his barque glide down the bay,
    Through tears and fears she could not banish;
She saw his white sails melt away—
    She saw them fade, she saw them vanish.

And 'Go,' she said, 'for winds are fair,
    And love and blessing round you hover;
When you sail backward through the air,
    Then I will trust the word of lover.'

Still ebbed, still flowed, the tide of years,
    Now chilled with snows, now bright with roses,
And many smiles were turned to tears,
    And sombre morns to radiant closes.

And many ships came sailing by,
    With many a golden promise freighted;
But nevermore from sea or sky
    Came love to bless her heart that waited.

Yet on, by tender patience led,
    Her sacred footsteps walked unbidden,
Wherever sorrow bowed its head,
    Or want and care and shame were hidden.

And they who saw her snow-white hair,
    And dark sad eyes so deep with feeling,
Breathed all at once the chancel air,
    And seemed to hear the organ pealing.

Till once, at shut of autumn day,
    In marble chill she paused and hearkened,
With startled gaze where far away
    The wastes of sky and ocean darkened.

There for a moment, faint and wan,
    High up in air, and landward striving,
Stern-fore a spectral barque came on,
    Across the purple sunset driving.

Then something out of night she knew,
    Some whisper heard, from heaven descended,
And peacefully as falls the dew
    Her long and lonely vigil ended.

The violet and the bramble-rose
    Make glad the grass that dreams above her;
And, freed from time and all its woes,
    She trusts again the word of lover.

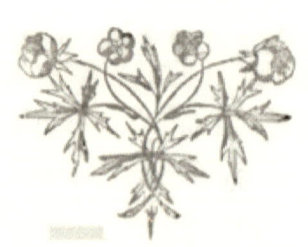

VIOLET.

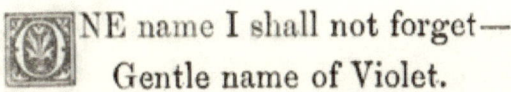

ONE name I shall not forget—
  Gentle name of Violet.

Many and strange the years have sped;
She who bore that name is dead;

Dead—and resting by the sea,
Where she gave her heart to me.

Dead—and now the grasses wave,
And the dry leaves, o'er her grave,

Rustling in the autumn wind,
Like the sad thoughts in my mind.

She was light, and soon forgot;
Loved me well, and loved me not.

Changeful as the April sky—
Kind or cruel, sad or shy;

Gray-eyed, winsome, arch, and fair—
My youth's passion and despair.

Now, through storms of many years,
Now, through tender mist of tears,

Looking backward, I can see
She was always true to me.

Yet, with prisoned tears that burn,
Cold we parted, wayward, stern;

Spoke the quiet, farewell word,
Neither meant and neither heard,

Spoke—and parted in our pain,
Nevermore to meet again.

Sometimes, underneath the moon,
On rose-laden nights of June,—

When white clouds drift o'er the blue,
And the pale stars glimmer through,

And the honeysuckle throws
Fragrant challenge to the rose,

And the liberal pine-tree flings
Perfume on the midnight's wings,—

Came, with thrills of hope and fear,
Mystic sense that she was near;

Came the thought,—Through good and ill
She loves, and she remembers still!

But no word e'er came or went;
And, when nine long years were spent,

Something in my bosom said,
Very softly,—She is dead!

Now, at sombre autumn eve,
Wandering where the woodlands grieve,

Or where wild winds whistle free,
On the hills that front the sea,

Cruel thoughts of love and loss
Nail my spirit to the cross.

Friends have fallen, youth is gone,
Fields are brown and skies are wan:

One name I shall not forget—
Gentle name of Violet.

A DIRGE.

March 4, 1874.

SPRING will return, and woods grow green
    From shore to shore;
But she, unseeing and unseen,
    Returns no more.

Low in the ground her sleep is sweet,
    And dark, and long:
No more she treads, with wandering feet,
    Our maze of wrong.

No more the world's rebuke can fret
    Her soul's repose;
Nor kindness woo her to forget
    Her bitter woes.

She will not stir, nor speak, nor heed,
    Though eyes that weep,
And sorrow-stricken hearts that bleed
    Beseech her sleep.

Yet be it mine, above her pall,
  To shed one tear;
And speak one word of love, that all
  The world may hear.

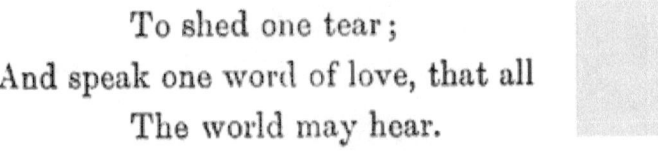

A brother's place in that fond breast
  'Twas mine to hold:
Ah, they loved most who knew her best—
  That heart of gold.

She was more kind than morning light
  To eyes that grieve;
And constant as the star of night,
  That can't deceive.

There was no sorrow on this earth
  But touched her heart;
And in all gentle childlike mirth
  She bore her part.

There was no goodness, but it won
  Her reverent praise;
And full of kind deeds, simply done,
  Were all her days.

She strove, through trouble's lasting blight,
  For pathways smooth;
And many hands she found to smite,
  And few to soothe.

A child, whom cruel want has made
    A thing forlorn,
Stretching its little hands, for aid,
    To eyes that scorn;

And wandering through the winter night,
    For beggar's dole,
Is not more piteous in its plight
    Than was her soul.

Yet did she hope and toil, and wait
    Heaven's will to know,
Till came the awful stroke of fate
    That laid her low.

Sleep softly, softly, true and tried,
    Where troubles cease;
And take at last, what man denied,
    God's gift of peace.

THEIR STORY.

I.

THEY walked beside the summer sea,
    And watched the slowly dying sun;
And 'O,' she said, 'come back to me,
    My love, my own, my only one!'
But while he kissed her fears away,
    The gentle waters kissed the shore,
And, sadly whispering, seemed to say,
    He'll come no more! he'll come no more!

II.

Alone beside the autumn sea
    She watched the sombre death of day;
And 'O,' she said, 'remember me,
    And love me, darling, far away!'
A cold wind swept the watery gloom,
    And, darkly whispering on the shore,
Sighed out the secret of his doom,—
    He'll come no more! he'll come no more!

III.

In peace beside the winter sea,
    A white grave glimmers in the moon;
And waves are fresh, and clouds are free,
    And shrill winds pipe a careless tune.
One sleeps beneath the dark blue wave,
    And one upon the lonely shore;
But, joined in love, beyond the grave,
    They part no more! they part no more!

EBB TIDE.

N dusky gloom she sits apart,
    Beyond the moonlight's silver glow,
And tender fancies break her heart,
    That bloomed and withered long ago.

Her patient eyes are wet with tears,
    Her face is pale with want and care,
And all the griefs of all her years,
    Transfigured, crown her snowy hair.

Gaunt sorrow claims her, heart and brain;
    She bears the burden of the cross;
She hears a solemn dirge of pain,
    The sad old song of love and loss.

So glide the lonesome hours away;
    The song is still, the grief is past:
Alike to her are night and day—
    The poor frail body rests at last.

IN A CHURCHYARD.

THE lonesome wind of Autumn grieves;
    The northern lights are seen;
October sheds her changing leaves
    Upon the churchyard green,
Where, sitting pensive in the sun,
    While fading grasses wave,
I watch the crickets leap and run
    Upon a stranger's grave.

There is no sigh of fluttering leaf,
    No sob of rustling grass;
The breezes o'er this place of grief
    In breathless whisper pass;
Yet, like a murmur in a dream,
    Purls on that insect voice—
That vacant tone which does not seem
    To mourn or to rejoice.

A tone that hath no soothing grace,
    A tone that nothing saith,
A tone that's like this solemn place
    Of memory, tears, and death—

It darkens hope, it deepens gloom,
 Black fear, and doubt profound,
Turning the silence of the tomb
 To more mysterious sound.

There's night upon the face of fame;
 There's night on beauty's eyes;
Nor pure renown nor glorious shame
 From out their ashes rise:
In vain the shrines of prayer are trod—
 Nor sound nor silence breathe
The thought that flowers upon this sod,
 The secret hid beneath.

Ah, piteous, desolate, and drear
 This nameless stranger's sleep,
O'er which the slowly dying year
 Is all that seems to weep.
God help him in that bitter day,—
 His heart, his reason save,—
Who hears the crickets chirp, at play,
 Upon his darling's grave!

AFTER LONG YEARS.

DEAR heart and true, in the seasons fled,
    Has the world swept by me and left me
        dead?

Have the pansies withered I used to know?
Are the roses faded of Long Ago?

Do the tapers glimmer that lit the feast?
Has the pageant passed? has the music ceased?

And, musing here on the sea-beat coast,
Am I living man, or a wandering ghost?

Still, in the scent of the autumn air
I feel a rapture that's like despair:

The starlight, pale on the sleeping sea,
Is a nameless, sorrowful joy to me:

And, lit by orb or crescent of night,
Meadow and woodland are brave to sight.

Still I bend to the mystic power
Of the strange sea-breeze and the breath of flower;

And the face of beauty wakes the wraith
Of holy passion and knightly faith!

But ever I hear an undertone—
A subtle, sorrowful, wordless moan ;

The dying note of a funeral bell ;
The faltering sigh of a last farewell :

And ever I see, through lurid haze,
The sombre phantoms of other days—

In light that's sad as the ruin it frets,
The solemn light of a sun that sets.

Ah, never again can youth dream on
As it used to dream in the summers gone !

For round it dashes the tide of years ;
Its eyes are darkened with mist of tears ;

Its hopes are sere as the fading grass,
And nothing it wished has come to pass.

But, O, it is wild in his heart, this day,
Who breathes a blessing and speeds away—

In trust, when the flags of triumph wave,
Where his soul is moored he may find his
    grave.

IN MEMORY OF GEORGE ARNOLD.

Greenwood, November 13, 1865.

BENEATH the still November sky,
  With Nature's peace and beauty blest,
We put our selfish sorrow by,
  And laid our comrade down to rest.

Rest—in the morning of his days!
  Rest—when his heart had just begun
To feel the warmth of all men's praise,
  The radiance of the rising sun!

Rest—to a strong and stately mind,
  That rose all common flights above!
Rest—to a heart as true and kind
  As ever glowed with human love!

And round him, dimly, through our grief,
  In every natural sound we heard—
In whispering grass, and rustling leaf,
  And sighing wind—the same sweet word:

Rest! And we did not break the spell,
 By holy Nature woven round
The fading form we left to dwell
 For ever in her hallowed ground.

No hymns were sung, no prayers were said,
 Save what our loving hearts could say,
When, mutely gazing on the dead,
 We blessed him ere we turned away:

Back to the round of daily care
 That seems so vacant to us now,
Remembering what repose was there,
 What peace, upon his marble brow.

And so we left him,—nevermore
 To see, in sunshine or in rain,
The semblance of the form he wore—
 Whose loss has steeped our souls in pain.

But, long as skies of autumn smile,
 And long as clouds of autumn weep,
Or autumn leaves their splendours pile
 In sorrow o'er their poet's sleep;

And long as violets grace the spring,
 Or June-born roses blush and blow,
Or pale stars shine, or south winds sing,
 Or tides of summer ebb and flow;

So long shall live their poet's name,
  When rest these broken hearts of ours,—
Embalmed in love, surpassing fame,
  With stars and leaves and clouds and
    flowers!

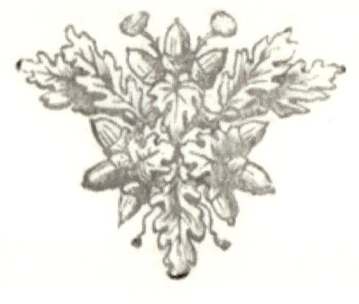

BEYOND THE DARK.

THERE'S a region afar from earth
    Should be very happy to-day;
For a sweet soul, ripe for its birth,
    Has gone from this world away.

And I think, as I sit alone,
    While the night is falling around,
Of a cold, white, gleaming stone,
    And a long, lone, grassy mound;

And of what rests under the sod,—
    The poor, pale face; the still brain,
Left awfully still by the spirit of God,
    That has gone to Him again;

The eyes that will shine no more,
    The hands that have done their task;—
And my heart is heavy and sore,
    And my mind is hungry to ask

If all, indeed, be well
    In the realms beyond the dark ;
What secret the pallid lips could tell
    Of that body so quiet and stark.

But there comes a murmur of trees,
    That wave their arms, and bring
Buds, blossoms, and leaves to shake in the
        breeze
    From spring to spring ;

And they whisper that all is well,
    For the same hand guides us all,
Whether 'tis seen in a man's death-knell,
    Or in the leaves that fall.

And so many have gone before,
    That the voice of another sphere
Floats often from over a sable shore,
    And pierces the mist of fear.

O tender heart that is still,
    You will falter with trouble no more,
Nor know of the good or the ill
    Of a frantic world's uproar !

Nor heed the great or the small
    Of a strange, bewildering life,
That often seems dust and ashes all,
    And is mostly a vapid strife.

For the end is the peace of grass,
    And God's peace, ever to be:
The one for us to feel as we pass,
    The other enshrining thee.

Clouds sail, and waters flow,
    And our souls must journey on;
But it cannot be ill to go
    The way that thou hast gone.

THE apples are ripe in the orchard,
    The work of the reaper is done,
And the golden woodlands redden
    In the blood of the dying sun.

At the cottage-door the grandsire
    Sits, pale, in his easy-chair,
While a gentle wind of twilight
    Plays with his silver hair.

A woman is kneeling beside him;
    A fair young head is prest,
In the first wild passion of sorrow
    Against his aged breast.

And far from over the distance
    The faltering echoes come,
Of the flying blast of trumpet
    And the rattling roll of drum.

Then the grandsire speaks, in a whisper,—
    'The end no man can see;
But we give him to his country,
    And we give our prayers to Thee.'. . .

The violets star the meadows,
    The rose-buds fringe the door,
And over the grassy orchard
    The pink-white blossoms pour.

But the grandsire's chair is empty,
    The cottage is dark and still,
There's a nameless grave on the battle-field,
    And a new one under the hill.

And a pallid, tearless woman
    By the cold hearth sits, alone;
And the old clock in the corner
    Ticks on with a steady drone.

BEAUTY.

I HAD a dream, one glorious summer night,
    In the rich bosom of imperial June.
Languid I lay upon an odorous couch,
Golden with amber, festooned wildly o'er
With crimson roses; and the longing stars
Wept tears of love upon their clustered leaves.
Above me soared the azure vault of heaven,
Vast and majestic; cinctured with that path
Whereby, perchance, the sea-born Venus found
Her way to higher spheres; that path which seems
A coronet of silver, gemmed with stars,
And bound upon the forehead of young Night.
There, as I lay, the musical south wind
Shook all the roses into murmurous life,
And poured their fragrance o'er me in a shower
Of crimson mist; and softly, through the mist,
Came a low, sweet, enchanting melody,
A far-off echo from a land of dreams,
Which with delicious languor filled the air,
And steeped in bliss the senses and the soul.

Then rose a shape, a dim and ghostly shape,
Whereto no feature was, nor settled form,
A shadowy splendour, seeming as it came
A pearly summer cloud shot through and through
With faintest rays of sunset; yet within
A spirit dwelt; and, floating from within,
A murmur trembled sweetly into words:—

I am the ghost of a most lovely dream,
Which haunted, in old days, a poet's mind.
And long he sought for, wept, and prayed for me;
And searched through all the chambers of his soul,
And searched the secret places of the earth,
The lonely forest and the lonely shore;
And listened to the voices of the sea,
What time the stars shone out, and midnight cold
Slept on the dark waves whispering at his feet;
And sought the mystery in a human form,
Amid the haunts of men, and found it not;
And looked in woman's fond, bewildering eyes,
And mirrored there his own, and saw no sign:
But only in his sleep I came to him,
And gave him fitful glimpses of my face,
Whereof he after sang in sweetest words;
Then died, and came to me.   But evermore,
Through lonely days and wakeful, haunted nights,
A life of starlit gloom, do poets seek

To rend the mystic veil that covers me,
And evermore they grasp the empty air.
For only in their dreams I come to them,
And give them fitful glimpses of my face,
And lull them, siren-like, with words of hope—
That promise, some time, to their ravished eyes,
Beauty, the secret of the universe,
God's thought, that gives the soul eternal peace.

Then the voice ceased, and only, through the mist,
The shaken roses murmured, and the wind.

OLD TIMES.

R OSY days of youth and fancy,
    Happy hours of long ago!
Ah, the playful pictured memories!
    Let us catch them as they flow.

Galaxies of blue-eyed Marys,
    With a Julia and a Jane,
And a troop of little Lauras,
    Blush and laugh and romp again.

Moonlight meetings, evening rambles,
    When the night was still around,
And a sweet voice, softly murmuring,
    Or a kiss the only sound.

These remember; and remember
    How the kind stars shone above,
Keeping, in their mellow splendour,
    Watch and ward upon our love.

Youth is as a diamond dawning—
    Bold it breaks to gorgeous day;
Heavenly lights of power and beauty
    Glance and gleam along its way.

Far within the mighty future
    There be solemn voices heard!
Shaped to many a stately anthem
    Floats the music of a word.

But that music, in the present,
    Softly droops, with sad decay,
Till its echo, in the spirit,
    Faints, and fails, and dies away.

Green be then the tender memory
    Of the past, for ever sped;
So that youth may be immortal,
    Though its days and dreams are dead.

EGERIA.

THE star I worship shines alone,
    In native grandeur set apart ;
Its light, its beauty, all my own,
    And imaged only in my heart.

The flower I love lifts not its face
    For other eyes than mine to see ;
And, having lost that sacred grace,
    'Twould have no other charm for me.

The hopes I bear, the joys I feel,
    Are silent, secret, and serene ;
Pure is the shrine at which I kneel,
    And Purity herself my Queen.

I would not have an impious gaze
    Profane the altar where are laid
My hopes of nobler, grander days,
    By heaven inspired, by earth betrayed.

I would not have the noontide sky
    Pour down its bold, obtrusive light
Where all the springs of feeling lie,
    Deep in the soul's celestial night.

Far from the weary strife and noise,
    The tumult of the great To-Day,
I guard my own congenial joys,
    And keep my own sequestered way.

For all that world is cursed with care;
    Has nothing holy, nothing dear,
No light, no music anywhere,—
    It will not see, it will not hear.

But thou, sweet Spirit, viewless Power,
    Whom I have loved and trusted long,—
In pleasure's day, in sorrow's hour,—
    Muse of my life and of my song;

Breathe softly, thou, with peaceful voice,
    In my soul's temple, vast and dim!
In thine own perfect joy rejoice,
    With morning and with evening hymn!

And though my hopes around me fall
    Like rain-drops in a boundless sea,
I will not think I lose them all
    While yet I keep my trust in thee!

THE MERRY MONARCH.

I.

T comes into my mind,—in a genial mood,
    When the worlds of my being, without
        and within,
Are quietly happy in all that is good,
    Unclouded by care and untempted by sin,—
If the gods would but grant me my dearest desire,
    As I fancy, sometimes, they're inclining to do,
That I shouldn't sit here, looking into the fire,
    And dreaming, my love, as I'm dreaming of you.

II.

Nor should I be thinking, as sometimes I am,—
    If the gods had but made me the thing I
        would be,—
That a station of rank, in a world full of sham,
    Were a pleasant and suitable station for me.
Nor should I be striving, with heart and with brain,
    For the laurel that poets are anxious to wear,—
That dubious guerdon for labour and pain,
    That sorry exchange for the natural hair.

E

III.

No ! I never should care, if I had my own way,
 For the storm or the sunshine, the Yes or the
  No;
But, quietly careless and perfectly gay,
 I could let the world go as it wanted to go.
I should ask neither riches, nor station, nor power;
 They are chances, they happen, and there is
  an end;
But a heart that beats merrily every hour
 Is a god's richest gift, is a man's truest friend.

IV.

And that's what I'd have! For that blessing I
 pray!
 A spirit so gentle and easy and bright,
It should gladden with sunshine the sunniest day,
 And with magical splendour illumine the night.
I could envy no potentate under the sun,
 However sublime might that potentate be;
For I'd live, the illustrious Monarch of Fun,
 And the rest of the world should be happy
  with me.

V.

I'd be gold in the sunshine and silver in showers;
 I'd be rainbows, and clouds all of purple and
  pearl;

And the fairies of fun should laugh out of the
 flowers,
 And the jolly old earth should be all in a whirl!
The brooks should trill music, the leaves dance
 in glee,
 And old ocean should bellow with surly de-
 light:
O, but wouldn't it be a tempestuous spree
 If the gods did but grant me my kingdom
 to-night!

VI.

And I think it will come,—that succession of
 mine,
 That crown with the opals of jollity set;
And the joy in my soul will be something divine
 When I finally teach myself how to forget;
Forget all of sorrow in which I've a part,
 All the dreams that allure and the hopes that
 betray,—
Contented to wait, with a right merry heart,
 For a home, and a grave, at the end of the
 play.

MY PALACES.

THEY rose in beauty on the plains
    Through which my childhood danced in
        glee,
When roses wreathed my idle chains,
    And holy angels talked with me.

They rose sublime on mountain heights
    Whereto my ardent youth aspired,—
Through silver days and golden nights,
    Ere yet my heart grew dull and tired.

Their stately towers were all aflame
    With rosy hues of morning light;
For hope and love and power and fame
    Burned on their peaks and made them bright.

Now, brown and level fields expand
    Around me, as I hold my way
Through barren hills on either hand,
    And under skies of sober gray.

No radiant towers in distance rise,
    On soaring mountains strong and glad;
No gorgeous banners flaunt the skies,—
    But all the scene is calm and sad.

Yet here and there, along the plain,
    A flower lights up the fading grass;
And whispering wind and rustling rain
    Make gentle music as I pass.

And now and then a happy face,
    And now and then a merry thought,
Give to the scene a pensive grace,
    The sweeter that it comes unsought.

And, looking past all earthly ill,
    I know there comes an hour of rest,—
In a dark palace, lowly, still,
    And sacred to the weary guest.

AT PEACE.

Staten Island, Autumn of 1873.

GREEN trees and quiet fields and sunset light,
　　With holy silence, save for rippling leaves
And birds that twitter of the coming night,
　　Calling their mates, beneath my cottage eaves—
These Fate hath granted for a little space
　　To be companions of my pilgrimage,
Filling my grateful heart with Nature's grace.

Not unremembered here the garish stage,
　　Nor the wild city's uproar, nor the race
For gain and power in which we all engage ;
　　But here remembered dimly, in a dream,
As something fretful that hath ceased to fret—
　　Here, where time lapses like a gentle stream,
Hid in the woodland's heart, and I forget
　　To note its music and its silver gleam.

But never, never let me cease to know,
　　O whispering woods and daisy-sprinkled grass,

The beauty and the peace that you bestow,
   When the wild fevers of ambition pass,
And the worn spirit, in its gloom and grief,
Sinks on your bosom, and there finds relief.

THE VEILED MUSE.

SPIRIT of Beauty, haunt me not!
    Thou bring'st insufferable pain.
Thou, who art gone, be thou forgot,
    Nor rise to vex my rest again,
Either with memories sadly sweet
Or hopes foredoomed to dull defeat.

Ah, come no more in rustling leaves,
    Or peaceful grass, or breath of flowers!
Enough this baffled spirit grieves,
    Remembering thee and rosy hours:
Spare it the throbs of hope and fear—
The cruel sense that thou art near.

The passion dies within my soul;
    The music dies within my brain,
Save when there comes a funeral toll—
    A low, lamenting, sad refrain,
An echo from that shrine of song
Long darkened and deserted long.

In what was fair I once had part,
    But all fair things are now my shame;
Their nameless beauty hurts my heart,
    Because I cannot speak its name.
Spoken, 'twould make that heart rejoice;
But, O, I cannot give it voice.

Once in these veins the blood was warm;
    With ardent hope this heart beat high;
And the great gales that proudly storm
    The loftiest ramparts of the sky
Were not more daring, fierce, and strong
Than this now silent soul of song.

But wasted now that youth of gold,
    Through mortal being's battered sieve,
And he to die may well be bold
    Who is not bold enough to live—
In haunted silence of disgrace,
Where hushed thy voice and veiled thy face.

Ah, come no more to do me wrong,
    In twilight hours of tender dream,
When this worn nature seems less strong
    Than evening mist that shrouds the stream.
Though love be dead, at least retain
Some pity for thy lover's pain:

Remembering still, though all be past,
    That thou and I clasped hands in youth :
I saw thee close, I held thee fast,
    Plucked kisses from thy rosy mouth—
Learning that bliss which now I weep,
The love J won, but could not keep.

LETHE.

I.

SWEET oblivion, blood of grape,
   Let me take thy hue and shape
Flood this weary heart of mine!
Turn it into ruddy wine!
Through my veins, with golden glow,
Airy spirit, flash and flow!
Deify this clod of clay,
And waft my willing soul away!

II.

Dark and sad my fancies are,—
Tired of peace and tired of war.
Joke of jester, prank of clown
Weigh my heavy eyelids down.
All philosophies are drear;
Music's jargon in my ear;
Endless tides of empty talk
Bubble round me where I walk;
I am deafened by the din
That the world is wrangling in.

III.

God of sunrise, fiery wine,
Let me lose my soul in thine!
Close my eyes and stop my ears
To all a mortal sees and hears:—
Roll of drums and clash of swords,
Fretful snarl of angry words,
Church and state and bond and free,
Party, creed, and policy,
Tattle, prattle, laugh, and groan,
Crozier, sceptre, flag, and throne,
Garrulous and grand debate,
Which of moles is small or great,
Who shall be prayed for, who shall pray,
And what the agile critics say.

IV.

Sun of rubies, radiant wine,
Melt my being into thine!
So my dream of death shall bless
Memory with forgetfulness.
No more weary, wasting thought
On a past so folly-fraught!
No more dreams of love-lit eyes,
Silken hair, and tender sighs,
And wild kisses sweet, that shake
The frame of being!—poor mistake!

Nor that other, just as poor,—
Toil for praise of sage or boor;
Fire, that burnishes a crown,
Fire, that burns a kingdom down,
Fire, that ravages his breast
Who takes ambition for its guest!
But at last, instead of these,
Sunset cloud and evening breeze,
Holy starlight shining dim,
Organ wail, and vesper hymn,
Cypress wreath, and asphodels,
Gentle toll of distant bells,—
All that makes the sleeper blest,
In a bed of endless rest.

v.

When this farce of life is o'er,
Are we fretted any more?
Do they rest, I'd like to know,
Under grass or under snow,
Who have gone that quiet way
You and I must go, some day?
If they do, it seems to me
Happy were it thus to be,
Sleeping where the blackb'ries grow,
And the bramble-roses blow,

And the sunshine pours its gold
On mossy rock and woodland old,
While gentle winds and clouds of fleece
And rippling waters whisper—Peace!

VI.

Vain the fancy: nothing dies:
Falling water falls to rise;
Round and round the atoms fly,—
Turf and stone and sea and sky,
Vapour-drop and blood of man,—
In the inexorable plan.
All is motion: nothing dies:
Mystery of mysteries.

VII.

Royal road of blest escape!
Sweet oblivion, blood of grape,
Let me take thy hue and shape!
In thy spirit floating free,
I shall be a revery,
A flitting thought, a fading dream,
A melting cloud, a faint moonbeam,
A breath, a mist, a ghost of light,
To rise and vanish in the night,—
Unseeing all, by all unseen,
And being as I had not been.

THE WHITE FLAG.

I.

BRING poppies for a weary mind
    That saddens in a senseless din,
And let my spirit leave behind
    A world of riot and of sin,—
In action's torpor deaf and blind.

Bring poppies—that I may forget!
    Bring poppies—that I may not learn!
But bid the audacious sun to set,
    And bid the peaceful starlight burn
O'er buried memory and regret.

Then shall the slumberous grasses grow
    Above the bed wherein I sleep;
While winds I love shall softly blow,
    And dews I love shall softly weep,
O'er rest and silence hid below.

Bring poppies,—for this work is vain !
    I cannot mould the clay of life.
A stronger hand must grasp the rein,
    A stouter arm annul the strife,
A braver heart defy the pain.

Youth was my friend,—but Youth had wings,
    And he has flown unto the day,
And left me, in a night of things,
    Bewildered, on a lonesome way,
And careless what the future brings.

Let there be sleep ! nor anymore
    The noise of useless deed or word,
While the free spirit hovers o'er
    A sea where not a sound is heard—
A sea of dreams, without a shore.

II.

Dark Angel, counselling defeat,
    I see thy mournful, tender eyes ;
I hear thy voice, so faint, so sweet,
    And very dearly should I prize
Thy perfect peace, thy rest complete.

But is it rest to vanish hence,
    To mix with earth or sea or air ?

Is death indeed a full defence
  Against the tyranny of care?
Or is it cruellest pretence?

And if an hour of peace draws nigh,
  Shall we, who know the arts of war,
Turn from the field and basely fly,
  Nor take what Fate reserves us for,
Because we dream 'twere sweet to die?

What shall the untried warriors do,
  If we, the battered veterans, fail?
How strive and suffer and be true,
  In storms that make our spirits quail,
Except our valour lead them through?

Though for ourselves we droop and tire,
  Let us at least for them be strong.
'Tis but to bear familiar fire;
  Life at the longest is not long,
And peace at last will crown desire.

So, Death, I will not hear thee speak!
  But I will labour—and endure
All storms of pain that time can wreak. . . .
  My flag be white because 'tis pure,
And not because my soul is weak!

F

DEATH'S ANGEL.

COME with a smile, when come thou must,
    Evangel of the world to be,
And touch and glorify this dust,—
    This shuddering dust that now is me,—
    And from this prison set me free!

Long in those awful eyes I quail,
    That gaze across the grim profound:
Upon that sea there is no sail,
    Nor any light nor any sound
    From the far shore that girds it round:

Only—two still and steady rays
    That those twin orbs of doom o'ertop;
Only—a quiet, patient gaze
    That drinks my being drop by drop,
    And bids the pulse of Nature stop.

Come with a smile, auspicious friend,
    To usher in the eternal day!
Of these weak terrors make an end,
    And charm the paltry chains away
    That bind me to this timorous clay!

And let me know my soul akin
    To sunrise and the winds of morn,
And every grandeur that has been
    Since this all-glorious world was born,—
    Nor longer droop in my own scorn.

Come, when the way grows dark and chill!
    Come, when the baffled mind is weak,
And in the heart that voice is still,
    Which used in happier days to speak,
    Or only whispers sadly meek.

Come with a smile that dims the sun!
    With pitying heart and gentle hand!
And waft me, from a work that's done,
    To peace that waits on thy command,
    In some mysterious better land.

DOOM.

A RAVEN flew over the house-top,
　　In the gloaming that heralds the night:
Far off snarled the threat of the thunder,
　　And the raven he croaked in his flight.

A raven flew over the house-top,
　　And his shadow fell dark on my heart:
A voice, in its innermost chamber,
　　Said, 'The angel of love must depart.

Too long you are calm in the sunshine,
　　And too long are the roses in bloom:
Time now for the rush of the tempest,
　　For the chill and the blight and the gloom.'. .·.

Deserted the house is and silent;
　　Even storm is too gentle to rave:
For Love, that made living celestial,
　　Is a spectre that dreams on a grave.

PREDESTINED.

A CALM, cold face, as white and clear
  As marble, and as passionless:
Eyes darkly sad, that tell no fear,
  No hope, no pleasure, no distress:

A smile, that seems o'er all to sleep
  As sleeps a sunbeam on a stone;
A quiet voice, but soft and deep,
  And full of music, every tone:

A courtly manner,—he is true
  To social usage, and will pay
To every one the proper due
  Of graceful, stately courtesy:—

Behold, an awful thought it is
  That such a ghastly, gaunt despair
Can wear a shape so grand as this,
  A face so noble and so fair!

For that is not a common grief
    Which tears his heart and burns his brain
Who feels eternity too brief
    For his tremendous trance of pain;

Whose soul endures infernal woes,
    Enchained by some infernal spell;
Who knows not peace, but only knows
    The lurid, withering fires of hell!

ACCOMPLICES.

BLACK rocks upon the dreadful coast,
    Mutter no more my hidden crime!
I hear, far off, your sullen boast,
    But I defy you! 'tis not time!

You cannot tell our secret yet;
    The trusty sea must keep its dead,
And many suns arise and set
    Before that awful word is said.

I am but young; I've all the grace
    Of life and love and beauty now:
There's not a wrinkle on my face;
    There's not a shadow on my brow.

I cannot bear the darksome grave!
    I will not leave the cheerful sun!
Rave on! in storm and midnight rave,
    For years and years, till all is done.

Till these brown locks are changed to gray;
　　Till these clear eyes are dim and old;
Not yet, not yet the fatal day
　　When all that horror must be told!

But, then—gnash all your jagged teeth,
　　And howl for vengeance! I will come;
And that same cruel pit beneath
　　Shall yawn and gulf me to my home.

To-day—forbear, nor mutter more!
　　The sky is dark, and dark the sea,
And all the land from shore to shore
　　Is hideous with your horrid glee.

ACROSS THE BIER.

NOW she lies here, dead before you,
　　Motionless and gray as stone ;
Now the cruel grief broods o'er you,
　　Stricken, agonised, and lone ;
Now that passion's dream is past,
Well it is we meet at last !

Ay, you loved her—loved her truly—
　　With the utmost faith of man ;
Sacrificing all things duly,
　　As a noble lover can !
And she made you—what I see ;
What 'tis well that you can be.

Loved her ?　Virtue, truth, and honour,
　　Sense, and manhood—what are they ?

Stand up here, and look upon her !
   'Tis a pretty piece of clay.
Others, quite as fond and true,
Loved her quite as well as you.

So I pity you, poor dreamer
   (Would to God our dreams were long !),
And I do not make it seem her
   Guilt that e'er she did me wrong.
She was heavenly—cloud and star;
She was what the angels are.

Hope and wait; and when you meet her
   With them, in the Eden plain,
Clasp her to your soul, and greet her
   With a word of noble pain.
Tell her, in yon starry cope,
That I taught you how to hope.

Time and tide flow on for ever;
   Pleasure's ghost is always pain;
Life is fevered with endeavour,
   Sad with loss, and sweet with gain.
But there is no certain bliss
In this world for only this.

Look up bravely where, forgiven,
    Erring hearts repentant rest.
Only love and trust find heaven!
    Still the faithful are the blest.
Faithful love, that ransoms you,
Well may save your idol too.

But for me there is no morrow,
    Crown of love nor crown of fame;
I must tread a mighty sorrow
    In the mire of sensual shame.
Down I grovel on the earth,
Wasting toward a brutish birth.

'Tis a world of commonplaces,
    Empty hearts and shallow brains,
Flaunting fools with specious faces,
    Black desires and crimson stains.
When I found that heart untrue,
Love itself was falsehood too.

Always round us are the curses,
    And the long, tumultuous roar.
We are jostled in our hearses,
    Even as we were before.
They alone escape the strife
Who attain the spirit's life.

Hope, I say, till you receive her;
    Hope, for we are only men.
Lay her in the grave, and leave her
    Just your heart, to keep till then.
Take my blessing—for I know
All your love and all your woe.

THERE'S a mossy, sunken grave,
  In the solemn land of dreams,
   All alone;
Where the dusky branches wave
  O'er the banks of sable streams,
   With a moan:
A dull sky spans it overhead,
   Like a tomb;
The wan stars glimmer far away
   In the gloom;
  And a pallid moon gleams
On the haunts of the dead,
Where the ghouls and the demons play.
  And the souls that wander here
  See each other very clear;
  And remember,—but weep not!
  Remember,—but sleep not!
   Remember,—but cannot pray!

LOVE'S RUIN.

THIS is the place where he brought her
    home—
  Home,—but not to his heart, I know:
For it cannot be but her memories roam
    To the first and the true love, long ago!
Noble and lovely and wretched bride,
  Doomed in her gorgeous palace of stone,
Loveless forever, to sit by his side,
    And yet be, for ever and ever, alone!

Noble and beautiful spirit of love!
  Well, I could wish you were happy,—though
I stand out here, while the stars above
    Are as white and cold as the ground below.
I am glad that the splendour is all your own;
  I do not desire it—ah, not I;
But am well content, at the foot of your throne,
    To lie down here in the street, and die.

Perhaps you would see me then—who knows?
  Perhaps you would see, in my haggard face,
Whence they have risen—your subtle woes,
  And the something that saddens your stately
    grace.
Perhaps—ah me, I am bold indeed!
  Perhaps you would touch me! Heart and brain!
I am sure it would make the old wound bleed,
  If it did not wake me to life again!

They say I'm a drunkard now, and a knave;
  That I riot and revel, by day and night;
And they're hoping, too, that I'll dig my grave,
  And get forever out of their sight.
'Tis a hard, hard world; but I think sometimes,—
  When I think at all,—could it only know
The bitter root of my follies and crimes,
  That it wouldn't be eager to hate me so.

No matter: I love you all the same.
  'Twas a faithful heart that you threw away.
I can say it now, and with nothing of shame,
  For I shall not live till another day.
I can say, though the night of grief was long,
  That the light of morning struggles through,
And, lifted out of my sorrow and wrong,
  If I cannot live, I can die, for you!

THE LAST SCENE.

HERE she slumbers, white and chill;
    Put your hand upon her brow;
Her sad heart is very still,
    And she does not know you now.

Ah, the grave's a quiet bed;
    She will sleep a pleasant sleep,
And the tears that you may shed
    Will not wake her,—therefore weep!

Weep,—for you have wrought her woe;
    Mourn,—she mourned and died for you:
Ah, too late we come to know
    What is false and what is true.

RUE.

THE autumn wind is moaning in the leaves,
    And the long grass is rustling on my
        grave:
Ah, would you have me think your heart now
        grieves
    For her you would not save?

For I am dead; know you not I am dead?
    Why will you haunt me in my grave to-night,
Standing above and listening overhead,
    Where I am buried deep, and out of sight?

Have you not wine and music, in your home,
    And her fair form, and eyes so pure and proud
With love of you? and wherefore do you come
    To vex me, lying silent in my shroud?

Seek your new love! She calls you, and the tears
    Are warm on her pale face, and her young breast
s full of doubt and sorrow,—for she hears
    Low-whispered words that startle her from rest.

In from the night! the storm begins to stir.
  I will be near, and ghostly eyes shall see
How you will kiss her lips, and say to her,
  'Thine always, love,' as once you said to me.

ROSEMARY.

'That's for remembrance.'

THE moonbeams on the water sleep
    In breathing light;
And tender thoughts and memories keep
    My soul to-night.

Shades of sweet hours forever gone
    Come all unsought,
And waves of mournful joy dance on
    The stream of thought.

A dreamy fragrance seems to rise
    From other years—
A solemn bliss that dims the eyes
    With happy tears.

Life wears the glow of rosy grace
    That once it wore,
And smiles are lit on many a face
    That smiles no more.

The gentle friends I used to greet,
All, all are here :
All forms are fair, all voices sweet,
All memories dear.

All happy thoughts, all glorious dreams,
That once were mine,
Rise in the tender light that beams
From auld lang syne.

But something in the heart is wrong,—
The joyous sway,
The spirit and the voice of song
Have died away.

These winds, that on their cloudy cars
Sweep through the sky ;
These wandering, watching, deathless stars,
My prayer deny.

These low, sweet murmurs from the land
And from the sea,
These waves, that kiss the silver sand,
Speak not to me.

And not to me one voice shall speak
For evermore,
Though the same waves in beauty break
On the same shore.

Shine stars, break waves, and murmur blast,
        And night-dews, weep!
To wait is left me, and at last
        The dreamless sleep.

THE VOICE OF THE SILENCE.

BEFORE THE SOCIETY OF THE ARMY OF THE POTOMAC.

Philadelphia, June 6, 1876.

BRIGHT on the sparkling sward, this day,
    The youthful summer gleams;
The roses in the south wind play;
    The slumberous woodland dreams:
In golden light, 'neath clouds of fleece,
    Mid bird-songs wild and free,
The blue Potomac flows, in peace,
    Down to the peaceful sea.

No echo from the stormy past
    Alarms the placid vale—
Nor cannon roar, nor trumpet blast,
    Nor shattered soldier's wail.
There's nothing left to mark the strife,
    The triumph, or the pain,
Where Nature to her general life
    Takes back our lives again.

Yet, in your vision, evermore,
    Beneath affrighted skies,
With crash of sound, with reek of gore,
    The martial pageants rise:
Audacious banners rend the air,
    Dark steeds of battle neigh,
And frantic through the sulphurous glare
    Raves on the crimson fray!

Not time nor chance nor change can drown
    Your memories proud and high,
Nor pluck your star of greatness down
    From glory's deathless sky!
Forevermore your fame shall bide—
    Your valour tried and true;
And that which makes your country's pride
    May well be pride to you!

Forever through the soldier's thought
    The soldier's life returns—
Or where the trampled fields are fought,
    Or where the camp-fire burns.
For him the pomp of morning brings
    A thrill none else can know:
For him night waves her sable wings
    O'er many a nameless woe.

How often, face to face with death,
　　In stern suspense he stood,
While bird and insect held their breath
　　Within the ambushed wood!
Again he sees the silent hills,
　　With danger's menace grim;
And darkly all the shuddering rills
　　Run red with blood for him.

For him the cruel sun of noon
　　Glares on a bristling plain;
For him the cold disdainful moon
　　Lights meadows rough with slain.
There's death in every sight he sees,
　　In every sound he hears;
And sunset hush and evening breeze
　　Are sad with prisoned tears.

Again worn out in midnight march,
　　He sinks beside the track;
Again beneath the lonely arch
　　His dreams of home come back;
In morning wind the roses shake
　　Around his cottage-door,
And little feet of children make
　　Their music on the floor.

The tones that nevermore on earth
    Can bid his pulses leap,
Ring out again, in careless mirth,
    Across the vales of sleep;
And where, in horrent splendour, roll
    The waves of Vict'ry's tide,
The chosen comrades of his soul
    Are glorious at his side!

Forget! The arm may lose its might,
    The tired heart beat low,
The sun from heaven blot out his light,
    The west wind cease to blow;
But, while one spark of life is warm
    Within this mould of clay,
His soul will revel in the storm
    Of that tremendous day.

On mountain slope, in lonely glen,
    By Fate's divine command,
The blood of those devoted men
    Has sanctified this land!
The funeral moss—but not in grief—
    Waves o'er their hallowéd rest;
And not in grief the laurel leaf
    Drops on the hero's breast!

Tears for the living, when God's gift—
    (The friend of man to be)—
Wastes, like the shattered spars that drift
    Upon the unknown sea!
Tears for the wreck who sinks at last,—
    No deed of valour done;
But no tears for the soul that past
    When honour's fight was won!

He takes the hand of Heavenly Fate
    Who lives, and dies for truth!
For him the holy angels wait,
    In realms of endless youth!
The grass upon his grave is green
    With everlasting bloom;
And love and blessing make the sheen
    Of glory round his tomb!

Mourn not for them, the loved and gone!
    The cause they died to save
Plants an eternal corner-stone
    Upon the martyr's grave:
And, safe from all the ills we pass,
    Their sleep is sweet and low,
'Neath requiems of the murmuring grass
    And dirges of the snow.

That sunset wafts its holiest kiss
    Through evening's gathering shades,
That beauty breaks the heart with bliss
    The hour before it fades,
That music seems to merge with heaven
    Just when its echo dies,
Is Nature's sacred promise given
    Of life beyond the skies!

Mourn not! in life and death they teach
    This thought—this truth—sublime:
There's no man free, except he reach
    Beyond the verge of time!
So, beckoning up the starry slope,
    They bid our souls to live;
And, flooding all the world with hope,
    Have taught us to forgive.

No soldier spurns a fallen foe!
    No hate of human-kind
Can darken down the generous glow
    That fires the patriot mind!
But Love shall make the vanquished strong,
    And Justice lift their ban,
Where right no more can bend to wrong
    Nor man be slave to man.

So from their quiet graves they speak;
    So speaks that quiet scene—
Where now the violet blossoms meek,
    And all the fields are green.
There wood and stream and flower and bird
    A pure content declare;
And where the voice of war was heard
    Is heard the voice of prayer.

Once more in perfect love, O Lord,
    Our aliened hearts unite;
And clasp, across the broken sword,
    The hands that used to smite!
And since beside Potomac's wave
    There's nothing left but peace,
Be filled at last the open grave,
    And let the sorrow cease.

Sweet, from the pitying northern pines,
    Their loving whisper flows;
And sweetly, where the orange shines,
    The palm-tree woos the rose:
Ah, let that tender music run
    O'er all the years to be;
And Thy great blessing make us one—
    And make us one with Thee!

IN MEMORY OF EDGAR ALLAN POE.

Baltimore, November 1875.

———

COLD is the pæan honour sings,
    And chill is glory's icy breath,
And pale the garland memory brings
    To grace the iron doors of death.

Fame's echoing thunders, long and loud,
    The pomp of pride that decks the pall,
The plaudits of the vacant crowd—
    One word of love is worth them all!

With dew of grief our eyes are dim:
    Ah, bid the tear of sorrow start;
And honour, in ourselves and him,
    The great and tender human heart!

Through many a night of want and woe
    His frenzied spirit wandered wild,
Till kind disaster laid him low,
    And love reclaimed its wayward child.

Through many a year his fame has grown,—
　　Like midnight, vast; like starlight, sweet,—
Till now his genius fills a throne,
　　And homage makes his sway complete.

One meed of justice, long delayed,
　　One crowning grace his virtues crave!
Ah, take, thou great and injured shade,
　　The love that sanctifies the grave.

And may thy spirit, hovering nigh,
　　Pierce the dense cloud of darkness through,
And know, with fame that cannot die,
　　Thou hast the world's compassion too!

GOOD-BYE TO BROUGHAM.

Lotus Club, N.Y., June 4, 1874.

——————

IF buds by hopes of Spring are blessed
    That sleep beneath the snow,
And hearts by coming joys caressed,
    Which yet they dimly know,—
On fields where England's daisies gleam,
    And Ireland's shamrocks bloom,
To-day shall Summer, in her dream,
    Be glad with thoughts of Brougham.

To-day, o'er miles and miles of sea,
    Beneath the jocund sun,
With merrier force and madder glee
    The bannered winds shall run:
To-day great waves shall ramp and reel,
    And clash their shields of foam,
With bliss to feel the coming keel
    That bears the wanderer home!

For he that (loved and honoured here—
　　God bless his silver head!)
O'er many a heart, for many a year,
　　The dew of joy has shed,
Longs for the land that gave him birth,
　　Turns back to boy again,
And, bright with all the flags of mirth,
　　Sails homeward o'er the main.

Ah, well may winds and waves be gay,
　　And flowers and streams rejoice,
And that sweet region, far away,
　　Become one greeting voice;
For he draws backward to that place,
　　Who ne'er, by deed or art,
Made darkness in one human face,
　　Or sorrow in one heart!

He comes, whom all the rosy sprites,
　　Round Humour's throne that throng,
Have tended close through golden nights
　　Of laughter, wit, and song;
Whom Love's bright angels still have known—
　　He ne'er forgot to hear
The helpless widow's suppliant moan,
　　Or dry the orphan's tear.

Where boughs of oak and willow toss,
　His life's white pathway flows—
With many an odour blown across
　Of lily and of rose.
His gentle life that blessings crown
　Is fame no chance can dim;
And we honour manhood's best renown
　When now we honour him.

Ambition's idols crowned to-day
　To-morrow are uncrowned:
Their fragments are of common clay,
　Strewn on the common ground.
But unto monarchs of the heart
　Are crowns immortal given;
And they who choose this better part
　Are anchored fast on Heaven.

Grief may stand silent in the eye,
　And silent on the lip,
When, poised between the sea and sky,
　Dips down the fading ship;
But there's one charm his heart to keep
　And hold his constant mind—
He'll find no love beyond the deep
　Like that he leaves behind!

H

So, to thy breast, old Ocean, take
    This brother of our soul!
Ye winds, be gentle for his sake!
    Ye billows, smoothly roll!
And thou, sad Ireland, green and fair,
    Across the waters wild,
Stretch forth strong arms of loving care,
    And guard thy favourite child!

And whether back to us he drift,
    Or pass beyond our view,
Where life's celestial mountains lift
    Their peaks above the blue—
God's will be done! whose gracious will,
    Through all our mortal fret,
The sacred blessing leaves us still:
    To love—and not forget.

HAND IN HAND.

J. L. T.

Lotus Club, N.Y., August 6, 1874.

I.

THE odour that all sense delights
    Enchants us most on summer nights;
And music, Nature's kindest boon,
Breathes gentlest underneath the moon;
For summer night and moonlight give
Quiet and grace, in which we live;
In which alone the prisoned soul
Finds, if not words, at least control,
And, for a moment, lifts us far
Toward realms where saints and angels are.
So friendship's soft and tender voice
Sounds clearest when our hearts rejoice:
For, when contentment warms the heart,
Selfish and sordid cares depart,
Dulness exhales—and in their place
Burns the rich glow of peace and grace.

And then we see each other clear;
The voice within the voice we hear;
And deep thoughts surge to eye and cheek,
Nor words, nor smiles, nor tears can speak!
The old love-ditties that were sung,
The whispered vows, when we were young,
The silken touch of fragrant tress,
The maiden's awful loveliness,
Starlight and sea-breeze, beach and spray,
The sunshine of some sacred day,
A mother's kiss on lip and brow,
The tones of loved ones, silent now,
The light that nevermore will gleam,
The broken hope, the vanished dream—
All these come thronging through the brain,
Till, half with joy and half with pain,
Our souls break loose from common things,
And soar aloft on angel wings;
Out of the tumult and the glare,
The fretful strife, the feverish care,—
To that great life of peace and grace
Which waits the suffering human race;
That larger life than sight or sound,
Wherewith God's goodness folds us round.—
This is the magic, this the power,
That thrills and crowns the festal hour!

II.

'Tis summer, and the moon is bright,
And perfect gladness rules this night,
And through our rapture, gracious, free,
A silver voice, across the sea,
In tender accents whispers sweet—
'Be kind to him whom now you greet!
At England's fireside altar-stone
His fame is prized, his virtue known:
To England's heart his name is dear;
To him she gives her smile, her tear;
She loves him for his rosy mirth;
She loves him for his manly worth;
She knows him bright as morning dew;
She knows him faithful, tender, true;
Her hope comes with him o'er the deep,—
With him to smile, with him to weep;
Ah, give him friendship that endures,
And take him from her heart to yours.'—
That voice is heard! By deed and cheer,
We give him loyal welcome here!
In Art's fair garden, where we stand,
We take him by the strong right hand;
In friendship's cup the pledge we drain,
And bind him fast with friendship's chain.

HAND IN HAND.

Honour the man, whate'er his stage,
Who wields the arts to cheer the age!

III.

Ah, comrades, if I could but say
(To point and close this humble lay),
What other voices float to me,
Across another, darker sea;
What words of cheer are wafted through
My fancy's realm, to him and you,—
A music then indeed might flow,
Should make your hearts and pulses glow.
For then would ring out, rich and deep,
The royal tones of some who sleep,—
The brilliant and the wise, too soon
Snatched from our side; in manhood's noon;
Ere Genius half her vigil kept;
For whom our hearts and Morning wept:
And these a welcome, without stint,—
My feeble words can only hint,—
Should give this friend and comrade, come
So far from kindred and from home.
But, this denied, I prattle on,—
The echo, when the music's gone;
With yet the hope that words well-meant
May find a grace for good intent,

With you, companions, tried and dear,
With him, the guest that's honoured here.
Nor will I think he views with scorn
These rhymes of welcome, lowly born;
These wild-wood roses, faint but sweet,—
In kindness scattered at his feet.

COMRADES.

G. F. R.

Lotus Club, N.Y., August 29, 1875.

I.

AT morning, when the march began,
　　And hope's strong eagle waved her wing,
Through banks of flowers the pathway ran,
　　Beneath the silver skies of Spring.

We heard the mountain torrents call,
　　Far up among the peaks of snow;
Our happy laughter rang through all
　　The peaceful valleys spread below.

Our hearts were glad, our faces gay,
　　We trod the slopes with careless glee,
And through the hill-gaps, far away,
　　Hailed the blue splendours of the sea.

We knew no peril, felt no fear,
　　Nor thought how swift the moments pass;

The sighing pines we did not hear,
    Nor our own footsteps on the grass.

But day wears on and night is near,
    Gray banners mingle with the gold,
Our ranks are thin, our faces drear,
    The sky is dark, the wind is cold;

We hear the roaring of the waves
    Of that great sea to which we tend;
Our thoughts are in the wayside graves,
    And on the solemn journey's end.

No more in vain the pine-trees sigh,
    Full well their mournful note is known;
No footsteps pass unheeded by,
    No more unheeded fall our own.

No more we hear the joyous cries
    Reëchoed back from vale and hill;
The light has faded from our eyes,
    The music of our youth is still.

II.

Bereft of many a friend of yore,
    Whom Fate and Nature set apart
To hear and heed forevermore
    The dead leaves rustling in the heart,—

How should I sing a joyous song
   Whose thoughts are where the cypress blooms,
And autumn afternoons are long,
   And silence dreams among the tombs!

Ah, Heaven is kind that gives me grace,
   Through good and ill, through toil and pain,
To hold in yet more close embrace
   The cherished comrades that remain!

He, dear to all, whose gracious fame
   Is goodness, bright beyond eclipse;
He, tried and true, whose honoured name
   Is in your hearts as on your lips;—

He shall not, in this royal hour,
   Lack words of mine, my faith to prove·
And, though they be not words of power,
   They shall at least be words of love.

His the light-hearted, cheery mirth—
   The snow-white bloom of blameless days—
Wisdom and grace and manly worth,
   An honest mind and simple ways.

His the pure thought, the spirit sweet,
   The wild-wood charm of graceful art,
The sadness and the joy that meet
   In Nature's own benignant heart.

Him fortune never taught to fawn,
    Want never sued to him in vain:
The word is spoken and is gone,
    The actions of the just remain.

By wings of deeds the soul must mount!
    When God shall call us, from afar,
Ourselves, and not our words, will count—
    Not what we said, but what we are!

Ah, be it mine, or soon or late,
    In that great day, in that bright land,
With him as now to take my fate,
    Heart answering heart, hand clasped in
        hand!

AN EPITAPH.
April 2, 1875.

———

WIT stops to grieve and Laughter stops to
        sigh
That so much wit and laughter e'er could die;
But Pity, conscious of its anguish past,
Is glad this tortured spirit rests at last.
His purpose, thought, and goodness ran to waste;
He made a happiness he could not taste;
Mirth could not help him, talent could not save;
Through cloud and storm he drifted to the grave.
Ah, give his memory,—who made the cheer,
And gave so many smiles,—a single tear!

THE SEER.

I.

ORDAINED to work the heavenly will
An angel cometh, sent from far;
And Nature feels another thrill,
And Love has lit another star.

II.

At sweetest rest
Upon his mother's breast
Heaven's little wanderer lies;
While that fond mother dreams of Paradise,
And talks with seraphs, looking in his eyes.

III.

Earth was more beautiful because of him.
In woodlands dim
Wild flowers were born;
And limpid purling brooks,
The poet's earliest and brightest books,

Spoke of a new delight
Unto the morn.
And in the night,
When fairies, sporting underneath the moon,
In airy glee
Made revelry,
Turning the darkness beautifully bright,
As brightest noonday in the heart of June,
Every wavelet laughed, and after
Seemed to chase its own delicious laughter;
Till spent
With emulous merriment
It sunk to sleep in some secluded, cool,
Translucent pool.

IV.

On meadows gemmed with daisies
The wild bee swooned, in mazes
Of languid odour, more bewitching far
Than Orient perfumes are.
All natural objects seemed to catch a rare and
precious gleam.
The little happy birds
Trilled out melodious words,
All indistinct, though sweet to mortal ears;
Such as the poet hears,
With joy and yet with tears,

In some ethereal reverie, half vision and half
    dream.
  Through breezy tree-tops jocund voices thrilled,
    And, deep in slumberous caverns of the
      ocean,
    Wild echo heard, and, with an airy motion,
Tossed back the greeting of a heart o'er-filled
With gladness, and that speaks it o'er and
      o'er
    Till bliss can say no more.
The waves that whispered on the silver sands
Told the glad secret unto many lands;
And the stars heard, and blessed him from
    above
    With golden smiles of love.

v.

Touched by the lightning of God's eyes
    He spake in prophecies;
Interpreting the earth, the sea, the skies—
    All that in Nature is of mystery,
      All that in man is dark,
    All that the perfect future is to be,
      When quenched our mortal spark,
    And souls imprisoned are at last set free.
Backward he gazed, across the eternal sea,

And on the ever-lessening shores of time
  Saw ghosts of ruined empires wandering
      slow.
    Then, looking onward, saw the radiant
      bow
Of promise, shining o'er a heavenly clime.
And thus he knew of life its mystic truth—
  Hope, the rich fruit of youth,
And that wherein all doubt and trouble cease,
  The fruit of patience, peace.

VI.

At last came death, a gentle welcome guest,
And touched his hand, and led him into rest.
Time paid its tribute to eternity—
A pure soul, ripe for the immortal day—
And earth embraced his ashes : cold their bed,
For now the aged year was also dead.
The winter wind shrieked loud, with hoarse
      alarms,
    The keen stars shivered in the midnight air,
And the bare trees stretched forth their stiffened
      arms
    To the wan sky, in pale and speechless
      prayer ;
Prayer o'er a new-made grave, where fairies kept
A solemn vigil, singing (and some wept) :

Speak softly here and softly tread,
   For all the place is holy ground,
Where Nature's love enshrines her dead,
   And earth with blessing folds them round.

He rests at last : the world, far off,
   Runs riot in her mad excess ;
But now her plaudit and her scoff
   To him alike are nothingness.

A true, sweet spirit this ! 'not good,'
   That blind world said.   He went his way.
Beloved, maligned, misunderstood,
   Till glory closed his sombre day.

He learned, in depths where virtue fell,
   The heights where honour may arise ;
He measured down the abyss of hell,
   He scaled the walls of paradise.

But all he felt and all he saw
   Taught only—what the wild bird sings—
That law is peace, that love is law,
   And lord of life, and king of kings.

LONDON : ROBSON AND SONS, PRINTERS, PANCRAS ROAD, N.W.

www.ingramcontent.com/pod-product-compliance
Lightning Source LLC
Chambersburg PA
CBHW022141020726
47496CB00008B/2498